BLUE NOTES

A.D. HEWITT

This edition first published in paperback by
Michael Terence Publishing in 2022
www.mtp.agency

Copyright © 2022 A.D. Hewitt

A.D. Hewitt has asserted the right to be identified as
the author of this work in accordance with the
Copyright, Designs and Patents Act 1988

ISBN 9781800943919

No part of this publication may be reproduced, stored
in a retrieval system, or transmitted, in any form or
by any means, electronic, mechanical, photocopying,
recording or otherwise, without the prior
permission of the publisher

Cover image
Copyright © SeaMartini
www.123rf.com

Cover design
Copyright © 2022 Michael Terence Publishing

Contents

BLUE NOTES 1

Synopsis 2

Chapter 1: Christina's Last Examination 3

Chapter 2: Loneliness 5

Chapter 3: Christina's Examination Results 8

Chapter 4: Singing Practice 10

Chapter 5: Recording Session (Tamley Studio) 12

Chapter 6: The Radio Interview 14

Chapter 7: A (Continental) Tour 17

Chapter 8: The Diners at the Luxury Beach Restaurant 24

Chapter 9: Christina Spends Precious Time With Her Nephew 26

Chapter 10: The Sessions 28

Chapter 11: A Holiday Abroad 30

Chapter 12: Christina's Times Alone 34

Chapter 13: Christina Reads a Bedtime Story to Grandchild 37

Chapter 14: The Concert 39

Chapter 15: The Recording 41

Chapter 16: The Children's Tea Party 43

Chapter 17: Christina Plays with the Grandchildren 46

Chapter 18: The Merry Grandchildren 48

Chapter 19: The Band's Discontentment at the Glamour Party 51

Chapter 20: The Beach House 53

Chapter 21: Pep Talk 56

Chapter 22: The Proposition 59

Chapter 23: The Wedding (Day) 62

Chapter 24: The Honeymoon 64

Chapter 25: A Christmas Thursday 67

Chapter 26: LA Residence 70

Chapter 27: Lenny's Breakfast Treat 72

Chapter 28: Christina's Values 75

Chapter 29: Christina Answers Questions 78

Chapter 30: Christina Broods for a Baby 80

Chapter 31: Nights and Days 82

Chapter 32: Children's Games 85

Chapter 33: Christina Picks up Her Daughter and Her Friend 88

Chapter 34: Country Dancing 91

Chapter 35: Precious Memories 93

Chapter 36: Christina's Deep Sentiment 96

Chapter 37: The Days with Children 98

Chapter 38: An Hour At The Beach 100

NIGHTLIFE ... 103
Chapter 1: Christine's Deep Reflection ... 104
Chapter 2: A Toast of the Wedding Anniversary ... 109
Chapter 3: The Time at an Hour at the Beach ... 116
Chapter 4: Religious Beliefs ... 118
Chapter 5: Nightlife ... 121
Chapter 6: A Private Location ... 122
Chapter 7: The Reconciliation ... 123

BLUE NOTES

Synopsis

Since a teenager, Christina dreamed big. She formed a band, a group called The BLUE NOTES. This is her story...

Christina wants to do other things in her life other than music like get married and raise a family. Then there's her daughter to take care of and look after. Followed by the Grandchildren whom she deeply loves and also the children she's emotionally attached to. Her expectations a fulfilment.

Chapter 1:
Christina's Last Examination

Christina one of the candidates entered the Examination Hall with all of the candidates sitting their Examination. This time this was Christina's very last Examination on her last day at school!

Christina failed her Examination that day. It was a sad time for Christina. Leaving the Examination Hall in a hurry. Christina did not say goodbye to anybody. She left school with two members of her Form. They sat the same Examination. Walking to the Bus Stop. They waited for their bus. They got the Bus.

Today was the very last time Christina ever saw her two members of her Form at Secondary School.

At home, Christina was exhausted and tired. She rested in bed for hours to recuperate. Christina was so sad it was her very last day at school today. Also, her very last Examination!

Christina felt so miserable and deeply unhappy. Failing her Religious Studies' Examination, she felt persecuted as a result of it!

During that summer Term, Christina knew she had failed all of her Examinations. Including music too. Her favourite subject. (Christina possesses a fine singing voice.)

She usually sings in a shower or bath to please herself. Christina is deeply emotional when she sings. Her voice is passionate. Her voice resounds and reverberates around the bathroom. The bathroom is steamy with condensation.

That night Christina was deeply sad as today was her last day at school. She reflects on her last day and last Examination.

Since Christina failed her Examination what will she do? Enrol for the Sixth Form or College? Perhaps resit her Examinations?

Christina has a passion for singing. Christina has the urge and incentive to sing. She may consider doing any recordings or demos of her singing voice.

During these weeks Christina suffered from depression. She suffered from her misery. She applied for a Saturday job at a Department Store. She was rejected. She sensed failure again. Both in her education and employment. That summer she sang. She practised her singing. Her voice became beautiful! Her voice (vocals) was soft, deep and breathy, her songs short and emotive. From her singing, Christina was so deeply emotional!

Chapter 2:

Loneliness

Christina was invited to Laurie's house. They both spent time together alone in the lounge. Then Laurie's Brother Andrew joined them for a short time.

Andrew appreciated his sister welcoming him to join them. He was deeply appreciative of his sister for allowing him to spend time with her friend.

"How is the weight training?" asked Christina.

Andrew flexed his right arm.

"It's good. It keeps me fit and strong," replied Andrew.

Laurie reached out and touched her Brother. She felt her Brother's biceps, his muscles.

"Feel that! He's got muscles," said sister loudly.

Christina felt Andrew's biceps and muscles. She had been impressed at his weight training which he does at the gymnasium at a Fitness Club.

"You should join a Fitness Club," urged Andrew.

"You should you know. It will keep you fit," prompted Laurie.

Christina object to their prompting. She was uninterested and unenthusiastic about joining a Fitness

Club.

"Not now. Not just yet. I have to do other things first. It's not a priority just yet."

"I don't know. I am not that enthusiastic right now," shrugged Christina.

Andrew rose and left them both together. Going out of the lounge. He re-joined his friend who came back from a sweet shop.

As there was now silence Laurie spoke.

"What are you going to do?"

"I don't know. I might sing," answered Christina.

"You should sing. You have got a really good voice," encouraged Laurie.

Christina cheered up at Laurie's compliment.

"Do you think so? It's awfully nice of you to say so."

"School over! I will miss everyone."

Christina sulked and frowned.

"I miss everybody too. I can't get over it."

Laurie sensed she had achieved.

"I have passed. I am sure of it. It's time to move on."

Christina envied Laurie for how she passed her Examinations. Christina failed hers!

"I will sing!" said Christina self-assuredly.

"You really ought to," encouraged Laurie.

"I will sing," smiled Christina.

"Sing me something."

"I can't. I am blue."

"Maybe some other time," suggested Laurie.

Christina wanted to be alone. Feeling embarrassed, humiliated and miserable.

Christina left Laurie alone downstairs. She retired to the spare bedroom where she spent the night. That Friday night which oppressive and depressing for Christina!

Chapter 3:
Christina's Examination Results

On one Thursday morning, Christina received her Examination results.

She opened the envelope and looked at her Exam slip. She found out that she failed all of her Examinations. She obtained fail grades.

She screwed it up and threw it in a waste paper bin. Supposedly her friend Laurie pass a few of her Examinations. She still didn't know how everybody else did. She would never know.

Christina felt badly shaken, disturbed, miserable and unhappy at her Examination results. 'A' Levels were out of the question. She probably would have to re-sit her Examinations.

Christina sat down on the armchair. Sitting in an uncomfortable position. She worried about her life. She lacked opportunities and prospects. She had to find a better perspective on her life. Nowadays it's just gloomy prospects.

Despite her misery. She did overcome her setback. She was humiliated, frustrated and embarrassed. Her friend Laurie seemed unembarrassed.

Laurie expected to pass a few of her examinations. Laurie narrowly failed certain subjects. Laurie was disappointed at failing her Examinations. Laurie seemed quite optimistic. At the Sixth Form, Laurie would probably re-sit her Examinations.

These days Christina avoided Laurie. A bighead! Christina was far too embarrassed, frustrated, miserable and unhappy. In a bout of depression, she remained housebound.

She did not even sing once during that time. Her voice was hoarse. She suffered from dejection, stress and strain.

Alone in her bedroom and garden, she contemplated for long spells. From her charisma from singing. She recovered from her setback. She felt rather more optimistic about her future.

Her friends and families encouraged her to sing. However, from some of them, she received a negative response and these individuals discouraged her from singing.

Christina was too determined to sing. To practise her singing regularly. The techniques of singing. Ultimately to sing live was an eager desire of hers henceforth in front of audiences.

Night and day Christina would press the play of a cassette recorder and sing when the music played.

Chapter 4:

Singing Practice

Christina remained alone in her house. Alone in her bedroom, Christina pressed the cassette recorder. She sang well. Her desire was to compete against professional singers and vocalists. Her ambition was to be the best singer and artiste.

She learned the lyrics by heart. Her musician friend wrote the lyrics and composed the music. She hoped Love in the Dark and Round the Bonfire would be successful. She wished Claudine every success with it as well as a few other tracks she composed.

In these versions all of the tracks are dull. On vocals Christina was promising. The Band loved her vocals. The singer was immature, her vocals girlish, her emotion childish, her bravura magnificent and beautiful with deep passionate emotion.

Christina rejoiced at having excelled at singing. Particularly these songs – tracks sublime and transcendent.

Christina prayed the group would be successful. A guaranteed success. They dreamt of stardom. They have been obsessed with the limelight. Indeed, it's an obsessive prepossession of theirs.

Christina's objective was to keep on singing well and

for her band to play their instruments well.

Some thought they were inexperienced musicians. Their intention was to get experience to play well together whenever they had the opportunity to perform. Their intentional motive was to be able to play live together. The Band were determined and competitive to succeed as artistes.

When things were mediocre, at times the group had been despondent and fatalistic in their outlook and frame of mind.

If their recording career was short, they would still pursue it in the music industry.

The Group had been rejected by Major Record Companies.

One day the group had been noticed once at a gig. A Manager signed them on behalf of Management. Their dream had come true! The Band had been signed. Their wish had ended up becoming a dream! The Band became overjoyed at getting a record deal. The group rejoiced. Now life was pretty sweet. A pleasant sweetness!

Chapter 5:
Recording Session (Tamley Studio)

The record company assigned the Producer to the Group. The Group look forward to working with their producer. At their recording session in a studio. The Band recorded tracks on two late afternoons and late at night.

Track 1. AROUND THE BONFIRE.
Piano, synthesiser, keyboard, bass guitar and lead guitar, drums, saxophone and strings.

Track 2. LOVE IN THE DARK.
Synthesiser, keyboards, drums, guitars, cellos and violas.

Track 3. LOVE DOESN'T STOP HERE.
Keyboards, synthesiser, drums, guitars.

Track 4. MY CONFESSION.
Guitars, synthesisers, keyboards.

Track 5. IT DIDN'T HAVE TO BE THIS WAY.
Brass, percussion, synthesiser, keyboards, guitars.

Track 6. WHY DID YOU HAVE TO GO AWAY?
Drums, keyboards, synthesiser, guitars.

Track 7. YOU SHOULDN'T HAVE LEFT ME.
Drums, keyboards, synthesiser, guitars, backing vocals.

Track 8. TOMORROW IF IT'S OVER.
Drums, synthesiser, keyboards, guitars, percussion.

Track 9. COME NOW.
Drums, synthesiser, keyboards, guitars.

Track 10. I SHOULDN'T SAY THIS.
Synthesiser, keyboards, guitars.

Track 11. DAISYCHAIN.
Synthesiser, keyboards, guitars, strings.

The recording sessions finally ended over two days and one night. The Group were relieved that their recording had ended. The Producer was world-class. The Producer praised them for their professionalism and excellence. The mixing itself took about six weeks. The professional Engineer was the best.

Very late at night, the exhausted band left Tamley Studio.

The Chauffeur in a limousine picked them up and drove them home.

Staying at a house the group were ever so happy and proud of themselves at their recording (sessions) at the studio tonight.

Their recording of the new album was a personal triumph!

Chapter 6:

The Radio Interview

In a studio, Christina was interviewed alone without her band. She was nervous about going live on air. The DJ asked questions. Christina answered the questions.

"What were your influences?" asked the DJ.

"I have listened to various artists. I love classical music. The sound of orchestrated music is so great. I love listening to it. Even the great composers."

"What was life like growing up?"

"I came from an ordinary working-class family. My friend is middle-class. I studied Sociology. The class system. It's something like social mobilisation."

"Isn't that sociology terminology?"

"That's right. I learned that when I was a student studying sociology."

"What will you do now?" asked the DJ.

"Go on Tour. Go to the studio. Make another studio album," replied Christina.

"You have been received well. Isn't that good!"

"We thank our fans. We thank everyone. It is truly an experience for me. I love it! I do hope it continues. I don't know what I'll do if it all ends," Christina expressed heartfeltly.

"What would you do?" asked the DJ.

"I don't know exactly. I don't think anyone knows."

"Is fame up there?"

"It's great. We enjoy it when we can," smiled Christina.

The DJ played a track from her album. Then the DJ asked another question.

"Where does your Tour begin?"

"UK then Europe."

"You have a gruelling schedule ahead."

"It's a pleasure. It will be hard work. To go on Tour will be great."

"Are you looking forward to it?"

"Of course. The UK Tour and European Tour," replied Christina.

The DJ played another track from her album. Then when that album track had ended, the DJ asked another question.

"Was it hard to get signed?"

"I say so."

"Tell me about Love Doesn't Stop."

"I click my fingers. It has a groovy beat. It is soulful. What's great about it is the melody."

"Are you a natural singer-songwriter?" asked the DJ.

"When I get the inspiration. I write a song. Compose one."

"Choose a track?"

"I choose a track from the Contemporary Artists. It's one of my early influences."

The DJ played the track that the Artist chose in preference.

Christina was overjoyed at listening to the track.

"If it all ends tomorrow, what would you do?"

"I'll travel the world. Yeah. Come back and make another album," uttered Christina.

"Your style is avant-garde. Your influence is classic music. You do have orchestration in your tracks."

"I love to hear strings. If I can. It makes it sound refined," smiled Christina.

"Time has run out. It's been a pleasure talking to you. Do come back and talk to us," thanked the DJ.

"Thank you for having me."

Christina was off the air at the radio station. Quickly, she left the studio. She overcame her nerves during her radio interview. With regards to it, Christina seemed pleased with her interview.

Chapter 7:

A (Continental) Tour

At the Worthington Club Christina and her band performed live. They played well. The Band were moved by how their fans sang their songs.

Christina a vocalist sang well. The Band express their sentiment and affectionate sentimentality.

The Band got great pleasure at performing in front of their fans.

Making recordings was also another highlight for them. The Band was electrified by the sensations of the atmosphere. The venue was romantic and intimate. It's a wonderful pleasure to perform in intimate surroundings such as a club.

The excited fans were close-up. They took pleasure in watching the Artists perform. Their enjoyable experience was pleasurable. (The Fans did belong to their FAN CLUB.)

Performing live that night was memorable. That Christmastime was unforgettable. A wonderful seasonal time!

On a lovely sunny day, Christina relaxed by the poolside. Sitting down by the edge of it. She felt enervated and prostrated. To occupy herself she spent time writing lyrics to a song. The members of her group relaxed by the terrace smoking and drinking.

Christina took displeasure at being in the company of her group. She avoided them wanting to be alone by herself. She was desirous as well as disappointed.

In a notepad, she wrote lyrics to a song. She tried to sing verses of her song.

MIDNIGHT (LOVE) CHARM

YOU DON'T LOVE ME
I LOVE YOU
LOVE YOU TILL LIGHT
TURNS TO DARK
LOVE YOU UNTIL NIGHT
MIDNIGHT LOVE

LOVE AT MIDNIGHT
WE LOVE TILL STROKE OF MIDNIGHT
MIDNIGHT LOVE
LOVE AT MIDNIGHT

WE DANCE TILL MIDNIGHT
YOU SLIP AWAY
RUNNING IN THE WIND
NOW YOU HAVE GONE
A MIDNIGHT DREAM

One of the band members took a look at what Christina wrote down in her notebook. Mark seemed pretty impressed at the lyrics. He was inspired by thinking of whimsical imagery and a midnight romance.

"I like it. Really. I can picture it in my mind. A dance scene at midnight."

"Well, that's good. I have made some progress," smiled Christina.

Mark was absorbed in deep thought.

"I wonder what the others think. Hey! Take a look at this!"

One of them got up from the terrace. Peter came out into the poolside. Peter took an obvious interest in what Christina wrote. Her lyrics were impressive.

"Hey! It's good. It's whimsical. I can just imagine the dance. The midnight dance," said Peter happily.

Christina took her notebook.

Christina felt buoyed up.

"Thanks. I am glad you like it."

"Keep it up. It's good," encouraged Peter.

"It's exciting," gasped Mark.

Christina got excited at the exciting imagery and romantic scene of a romantic dance.

Christina got up from lying down. She stretched her legs. Throbbing from cramp.

"I am going in. I'll see you lot later," said Christina impatiently.

Going in Christina found her elder sister in her bedroom. Christina lay down on her bed. Christina engaged in erotomania. Clara massaged Christina's body. Her back. Christina took pleasure from her sister massaging her.

"Your hands are so soft. You're so gentle," said her sister softly.

Christina felt her sister's gentle massage. She soothed from Clara massaging her. Her glossy tanned body was moisturised and lubricated. Christina felt narcissistic pride. Engaging in narcissism. Her attractiveness was an attraction. (A vocalist with a fine voice.)

Christina took pleasure from her sister's massage. She felt her sister's gentle massage and soft hands. Her sister's delicate touch. Christina felt relaxed, laid back and carefree. She cooled down and calmed down. She pacified. Feeling calmer and peaceful. Christina soothed from her massage. The masseur professional. The masseur rubbed lotion on her body. The masseur massaged Christina's body. Her back and legs. Her body was covered with a white bath towel.

Christina thoroughly enjoyed her massage. She took gratifying pleasure from it. She was gratified by her pleasurable massage. She took pleasure from her female erotomania, her sex. The erogenous areas of her body.

After the short massage. Clara a masseur left Christina according to her sister's wishes.

Within minutes her body was wrapped around with a white sheet. The linen light. Christina fell asleep. She slept for hours. Taking a siesta. Today it was so hot. The sunny weather was sweltering. The others took an afternoon nap too.

A few days ago, the group took a break from their Tour. In the lovely garden that fine day they performed live an acoustic set.

"Dream on! Who will take us on?" infuriated Mark.

There was no response from the rest of them responding. The group performed an instrumental. An ornamentation. Christina moved around the garden and made gestures. The gesturer graceful. The vocalist mimed. Performing the group were emotional, elated and euphoric. Their live performance was a euphoria.

Later that night Christina stayed in bed. She was tired. She still suffered from exhaustion and fatigue.

Suddenly Mark and Peter burst into her room. He held glasses while Peter held a bottle of Champagne. They both were full of wonder as they gave Christina their immediate attention.

Christina was still in bed. She stirred. Her cheeks rosier flushed.

"You look lovely," said Mark admiringly.

"Do I really? I still have got my make-up on."

Peter ogled Christina. Admiring the attractive redhead. Christina's voluptuousness showed in the light. The sight of her figure from a sheet pulled back and a continental quilt moved aside. Christina got out of bed. She stood up. From her slinky nightdress, her figure revealed itself. The sight of it was noticeable from the semi-transparent material of her nightdress.

Mark put the few glasses on a table. Peter poured out the already opened bottle of sparkling Champagne into three glasses. Standing the revellers made a toast. They celebrated together.

"Happy Holiday."

"Happy Times."

They each drank a glassful of Champagne. The merry-makers indulged in another glass of Champagne except for Christina who abstained from drinking another glassful of Champagne.

Mark and Peter both left Christina alone.

Christina got into bed again. She felt refreshed from drinking. Her thirst quenched.

Within a few minutes, Christina fell fast asleep. That night she dreamt. She had a sweet dream that continental summer night.

Chapter 8:

The Diners at the Luxury Beach Restaurant

At the beach restaurant, the Diners dined. Sitting at a reserved table. The romantic restaurant was beautiful. With air-conditioning and fans. The Diners gourmets and Epicures.

The Diners sat while waiting for their meal to be served.

They drank beverages. They enjoyed the pleasurable luxury restaurant. They heard the sound of the waves and tide. The electrifying sound of the crushing sea.

The other Diners there were Iberians and Spanish or holiday-makers. The señoritas were glamorous and the teenagers well-dressed and well-behaved.

Christina, Clara and Mark and Peter ate a stew. The seafood-rich, fresh and tasty. The thick stew tasted spicy. They all ate a candlelit meal. It was a romantic candlelight. They indulged in epicureanism.

The group had been talkative, excitable and romantic.

The aura was a romantic pleasantness. The niceness of it a luxuriousness.

They were calm, relaxed, merry and exuberant. Bursting out laughing. They were full of high spirits and good humour.

They relished the romantic night. Enjoying the wonder of it. Looking out of the windows. They marvelled at the beauty of the beach. They admired the view of the beautiful sandy beach.

Sitting alone together they wished they could have spent more days and nights in Paradise.

These days they weren't keen on working, but just spending precious time together.

At that present time, they all reflected on Midnight Dream (Love) and their conversation about the montage and about their deep reflection on it.

Chapter 9:

Christina Spends Precious Time With Her Nephew

Christina expected her nephew to come around. She waited for Jon and his Mother to come. To drop off her son. During her tour, Christina had been too busy. During that time, she had neglected her nephew.

As Jon entered the house Christina greeted her nephew. Welcoming him she embraced her nephew. Christina kissed him on his cheeks affectionately.

"My boy! How are you?"

"I haven't seen you for ages," replied nephew.

Christina held her nephew passionately.

"You're big! Let me take a look at you."

"How come Lena gets something and I don't," grumbled nephew.

Christina apologised for being neglectful.

"I am sorry. I will make it up to you. I promise. I'll get you something. What is it you want?"

"A toy," answered nephew.

Christina got a bad conscience.

"I promise you. I will get you a toy."

Jon burst out crying as he felt neglected and unhappy.

"They always get something. I don't!" blubbered Jon.

"Things are tough right now. I have to watch my finances," said Christina bluntly.

Christina felt deeply ashamed. She picked up her acoustic guitar. She played beautifully her guitar. She sang her nephew a nice song.

Jon stopped crying. He cheered up. He liked being with Christina. Jon was overwhelmed with affectionate love.

Christina spent time with her nephew. She enjoyed spending time with her nephew. She got self-satisfaction and pure joy at being with her nephew. Nothing else could compare to it. It's such a special thing being together with a member of her family. Her nephew!

Christina spent the day with her nephew. She played with Jon's toys, read a children's book and played cards and a board game.

During the remaining time, her nephew also helped Christina with gardening and horticulture.

Today they were too occupied doing various things at their past-time.

As her playful nephew spent time alone by himself reading a comic. Christina indulged in relaxation pleasure by the poolside.

Chapter 10:

The Sessions

The Band played well in their sessions. They performed well live. They played a few tracks. The live performance sounded relatively different from the original recording in the recording studio. The Band doing these sessions made such a difference from anything else they had done previously.

These sessions remained a great experience. One which was truly memorable indeed. They took a break from their Tour to undertake recording sessions.

They pleased themselves. They took pride. They had their ego. The megalomaniac's egoists.

They were determined to improve themselves as Musicians and gain recognition in the music industry. The group declared it a personal triumph and success. They proclaimed it and announced Tour dates.

One of their concerts remained a highlight, limelight and a triumph. The vocalist sang well. Commanding the stage with her bravura.

What was amazing about it was how she recovered from stage fright. The singer was charismatic. Her band played well in that intimate venue. Did the band possess charisma?

The fever pitch electrifying with all their fans

chanting, singing and screaming.

Back at their hotel. Every band member relived their memories. What a wonderful memory!

From being questioned they were coy, reticent and evasive answering questions. At other times they avoided any interviews which they eluded.

They all stayed in their hotel where they took their time to rest and recuperate. Avoiding the limelight!

They relived their memory of their memorable concert which remained a highlight for them. Especially an unforgettable one!

Chapter 11:

A Holiday Abroad

Sitting at the garden table on the patio, Christina, Peter and his wife joined in the conversation.

"What will you do if it all comes to an end?" asked Peter.

"That's a hard question. I really don't know how to answer it. What will I do? I have to think about it. How about you two?"

"I am in love!" said Patty.

"When it's all over. I will settle down and have a kid. I suppose that's what we will do."

Christina was aware of Peter the guitarist sleeping in a separate bedroom. His wife was virginal. He remained obsessive about his wife's chastity.

"Are you happy with married life at present. Peter, you don't have any regrets?"

"No. I am a married man. I love being married. I have never felt so happy in all my life. I am married to a lovely wife. What more can one ask for?" said Peter honestly.

Patty put her arm around her Husband and squeezed him hard.

"We are in love!"

"This married lifestyle it's not rock and roll is it," retorted Christina.

"I dare say it is. What would you do when it's over?"

"I like to still compose and write songs. Or should I be ambitious and write a book?" replied Christina.

"You can do that. You're intelligent. Why don't you? I think you should," encouraged Peter.

"What would it be about?" asked Patty.

"I don't know. I haven't decided," stuttered Christina.

"How about Mark?" wondered Peter.

"Mark will marry. Won't he?" stuttered Christina.

"Mark is a dark horse. No one knows what he will do. I think married life will suit Mark. How about you?"

Christina explained her intention.

"I will keep going on until the very end. Whatever happens now. It has been a wonderful experience. A dream!"

"Patty. What would you like to do?" asked her Husband.

Patty still had an unfulfilled aspiration.

"If I could, I'd like to travel the world. Explore it. Be a globe-trotter," answered Patty.

"That's a good thing to do. Going to new countries

is educational. Isn't it? Travelling abroad is interesting. A fascination. I would like to travel myself if I have the opportunity. Yeah, sightsee. Should I settle down first? What are my options?"

Keeping out of the sun. Peter came indoors. He took a nap. The shade felt cool.

Meanwhile, Patty and Christina sunbathed out in the garden. Lying down on sun loungers. After hours of sunbathing both women were suntanned. Their suntan looked rather lovely in the Mediterranean climate. On holiday they both relaxed together in a paradisiacal garden of sheer beauty.

During the late evening, Peter helped his wife cook. They invited guests around for dinner.

Christina took enjoyment from relaxing with their few friends invited for dinner.

Much later on Christina avoided and eluded them. She stayed upstairs. There in a small bedroom, Christina tucked their Grandson into bed. Singing to him. The lyrics of a nursery rhyme.

That night Christina stayed up late till the late hours of the night. Talking to guests until it was eventually time for them to leave to go home.

Christina stood by the doorway of the lounge. Christina patiently waited for Peter to come into the lounge. Peter's sexy, buxom wife stayed outside with her few friends. Patty amused herself by flirting with one of them she had been attracted to since that time at midnight. Patty's vibes and attraction attracted desire.

Meanwhile, Christina remained alone momentarily with Peter.

"Hey! What's the big secret?" asked Christina.

"My Grandfather adores his Godson. He loves him!"

"Oh! How wonderful!" exclaimed Christina.

"Steve is dear to my Grandfather's heart!" added Peter.

Christina slouched and yawned. She put her hand on her mouth, then she turned to face the window opposite. There the moonshine shone through the French windows. In the pitch-black, the moonlight shining made such a reflection in the beam. Down the garden, where the dark shadows were beyond.

Chapter 12:

Christina's Times Alone

After Peter and Mark drank beer and relaxed by the terrace. They both re-joined Christina alone by the poolside which was sweltering from the heat.

In mid-afternoon, the hot sunshine was hotter. The air breezy.

Christina lounged on the sun lounger. Enjoying her time of relaxation. It was another day off.

Christina took gratification from her narcissism. Her eroticism from her sex appeal and her thoughts of erotomania. Her body tanned. She got a dark tan from basking out in the sun. Her suntanned figure was lovely. (From most of her Tour Christina remained untanned, preferring not to have any sex appeal and to attract too much attention as a lead vocalist.)

Simultaneously Peter and Mark lay down on sun loungers on either side of a sun lounger which Christina laid on from the comfort of her position.

"When it's over. Will you get married?" asked Peter.

"I don't really know. My Mother insists on discipline. No hanky-panky. My parents discourage it and disapprove of it. I like to romanticise. I often wonder about marriage. I dream of getting married. Isn't it exciting! Isn't it every woman's dream? I have got you two. You two are fine. I am not looking for anyone. I love to read romances. I love to have a good romance. I love to dream of romance," said Christina excitedly.

"You will marry one day. Won't you get married?" asked Mark.

"I often think of marriage. I think of married life. I fantasise about being in love. A married woman. A good wife!"

Christina lost interest in her romantic conversation of romance. She attended to a running Grandchild crying.

"She's not here. I am supposed to be babysitting. You're here with me."

The other Grandchildren came out from a nursery. Coming outside they took displeasure from their boredom.

Christina wanted to entertain them. Christina picked up her guitar, and then she sang to the children. The excitable children got overjoyed at her singing. Her fine vocals.

The mischievous children cheered up. Their smiles were radiant. Their parents arrived to pick up their Sons and Daughters.

Peter and Mark left both together with the children and their parents.

Christina remained all alone. Christina stayed alone at the house. Christina lounged by the poolside for hours and spent the rest of the day indoors. She read a romance.

Chapter 13:

Christina Reads a Bedtime Story to Grandchild

Christina spent the day at home. During the course of the long day, she wrote lyrics to a good song.

She somewhat struggled to write good lyrics. The lyrics themselves did rhyme. Christina felt dissatisfied with what she had written. She did develop some good ideas.

Sitting on a garden chair. She put her notepad down on the ground. Feeling desirous again. She felt uncomfortable sitting down for a long time. She does have aspirations. Christina relaxed alone. She liked to be alone at home. Enjoying the comfort and privacy of her home.

Due to a change of plans. Things certainly changed when a parent dropped off a Grandchild at her house. With an obligation, Christina willingly spent time babysitting today. Steve was a good child!

The child was playful, cute and sweet. Christina was fond of Steve. She loved Steve.

Occasionally Christina babysat. She was committed. This child may have been a handful!

Christina got more pleasure and satisfaction from being with Steve than from doing anything else. Nothing else could compare to this. There was no comparison at all for a woman's love for a child!

Later that evening Christina tucked Steve into bed. Christina took the time to read Steve a bedtime story. He loved the children's storybook.

Within half an hour Steve fell fast asleep. Christina kissed the angelic child goodnight. Standing and admiring the child. Rejoicing at the loveable child. She felt overjoyed at the sight of his angelic face.

At once she left the bedroom. The beautiful child was sound asleep.

At times like these Christina preferred to be in the presence of this child rather than doing anything else. She got such great joy!

Christina did not explain the deep emotion she deeply felt for this child to anyone.

Chapter 14:

The Concert

In the dressing room, all of the band said a prayer before they left together. They all emerged from backstage. They all appeared out on stage to screaming Fans. The band performed live. The Band played tracks off their album.

Christina the vocalist sang well and all of the Musicians played well: Guitars, keyboards, piano, percussion, drums, synthesisers and strings.

During the performance, the thousands of Fans sang their songs as they waved in the air.

The band performed a collection of songs which included a medley, ballad, ditty, nocturne, and instrumentals. This performance was one of the best they had done. This concert was memorable. It remained an unforgettable summer.

After the band performed, the emotional band left the stage at once. Then they returned on stage to perform an encore.

The band were deeply emotional and passionate about performing. The Band deeply loved their Fans. They were tearful and deeply moved by their ecstatic Fans. There was such euphoria in the atmosphere. It was wonderfully electrifying. It was fever pitch.

This particular concert was a highlight for the band. They did cherish their unforgettable memory of this concert.

At the Hotel the band reflected on their fine performance. They were elated and euphoric. They also felt a tinge of sadness too. They loved their Fans. They deeply missed all of them again and again. Their young Fans.

"What will we do, when it all ends?" said Christina pensively.

"Let's cherish our memories. Never forget!" said Mark wistfully.

Christina became deeply upset.

"There will come a time when our Fans will desert us," said Christina unhappily.

Peter had a different mentality.

"Let's not think of it. Let's enjoy the moment. Let's think positive, shall we," answered Peter.

In a luxury suite, all the band stayed together for a short time. Then they left each other to go to their hotel rooms to recuperate and rest themselves. Tonight, they were staying overnight in a hotel.

Chapter 15:

The Recording

Peter a band member spent time with Christina. At present Christina fretted about her Fans. She got deeply upset, sad and depressed. Suffering from a bout of depression.

"What's wrong?" asked Peter.

"Where are they? I am losing all of my Fans," groaned Christina.

"Put it down," ordered Peter.

Christina disobeyed and took a swig from a bottle of beer. Peter felt deeply concerned for Christina. He worried about her. Peter took a bottle of beer from her. He empathised with her. The sympathiser showing sympathy.

"Don't cry! I know how you feel. I feel the pain too. I can't get over it. We never will."

Christina suppressed her tears. She choked back. She burst out crying.

"GO! Leave me!"

"Are you alright? Are you sure you are OK?" said Peter worriedly.

Christina grabbed Peter's arm and pulled him. "GO!"

"I will go. Call me."

Christina was relieved Peter had gone now. She took comfort from being alone. With deep sadness, Christina cried. She blubbered.

A few days ago, Christina overcame her bout of depression. She recovered.

During Saturday afternoon Christina resumed writing a song. She continued with it. She improved it. There in another room, the Pianist composed a nocturne. The professional musician was avant-garde.

He spent hours as he presided at the Grand piano composing. In a trance. He was soon lost in a deep reverie…

Ultimately it ended up becoming a beautiful recording at the recording studio. This record with string arrangements and fine vocals. (Christina's backing vocals were sensationally fabulous.)

To this very day this track, LAST DANCE remained their best work in their Discography.

Chapter 16:
The Children's Tea Party

In the lounge, Christina relaxed in silence while waiting for the Grandchildren to come round to her house. She expected all of them to come. Their parents coming to drop them off. When they all came in Christina attended to them. The Grandchildren and their friends played out in the garden. The children had fun when playing amongst themselves.

Afterwards, they all came indoors looking for Christina. Some of them wanted Christina's attention. The few Grandchildren do desire her parental love.

"All of you do come and sit down. Let me read to you a story," gestured Christina.

All of the children obeyed and sat down together. They all showed keen interest in the reader wanting to read. Christina read out loud to them a story. With interest, all of them listened. Most of them liked the story. (The Granddaughter preferred a Teenage romance. Teens are her favourite.)

After having enough of reading Christina decided to do something else. She entertained all of the children by singing to them. She played acoustic guitar and sang to all of the children. They thrilled at having been entertained. After all of the children relaxed together. Keeping out of mischief.

Earlier Christina organised the tea party out of obligation.

Later all of the children had a tea party out in the garden.

The children ate their tea, a bowlful of ice cream and jelly, a slice of sponge cake and cheese and cucumber sandwiches.

Within a few hours, later the Grandchildren and their friends were picked up by their Parents and grown-ups.

Standing outside the front door Christina waved goodbye to them as they all departed. Christina enjoyed her time with the children. She took such joy in being in the company of children.

Nowadays nothing else seemed to give her that joy except for her music which was an exception.

On the patio, Christina cleared up the garden table. She cleaned up the table. Peter popped in to see Christina.

"Well how was it?" asked Peter.

"It was a great time. I loved it. It's such a joy being with children. I can't describe the feeling. You can't beat the feeling. I love children. Apart from music nothing else gives me that joy. Music is my love. But being with children is something else. It's such a joy. Nothing in all the world can beat it. My love for children. The children's love for me! I may quit the music industry. I will look after children. That's what I will do. Be a kid myself."

Peter ended up at staying at Christina's house. He stayed the night. Respecting Christina's privacy, Christina preferred to be alone.

Christina relaxed until late in the evening. Then she bathed and went to bed.

Peter stayed up late at night talking to Mark. That summer night was enchanting.

Standing by the window. Both Peter and Mark looked out of the window. From the sight of the dark glowing garden there, it was an illumination. A glorious enchantment!

Chapter 17: Christina Plays with the Grandchildren

In the big country garden, the grandchildren stood by an oak tree. They played hide and seek. As Christina stood by the tree counting. The few Grandchildren ran off in the direction of the house. The Grandchildren hid inside the house. Christina went looking for them everywhere. She could not find them anywhere. The few Grandchildren hid downstairs.

Christina went upstairs looking for them. Meanwhile, the Grandchildren hiding got out of their hiding places. They ran outdoors. They ran to an oak tree.

Christina looking for them upstairs got impatient looking for them. She lost interest in playing this game. She gave up playing hide and seek. Christina came downstairs.

She came out into the garden. There she found the grandchildren waiting for her at the oak tree.

Christina gasped. "There you are. Where were you?" said Christina loudly.

"We were hiding downstairs. You didn't find us," said Anne.

"No wonder why I couldn't find you all."

"Shall we play?" said Richard impatiently.

Christina refused to continue to play hide and seek anymore.

"Certainly not!" frowned Christina.

Playing with all of the Grandchildren gave Christina such great joy. She remained a child at heart. She got such satisfaction from playing with all of the Grandchildren. Her experience playing with the Grandchildren was a great one!

Nothing else gave her that great pleasure. Christina doing babysitting was rewarding and satisfying. Looking after and taking care of the Grandchildren gave her pleasurable joy. Nothing else could compare to it to the joy of it!

The few Grandchildren grew up. She took pleasure in their company and their presence.

Today all of the Grandchildren spent a few hours at the country house. Then their parents came to pick them up.

That day Christina had a great time with the Grandchildren. She got much more joy, pleasure and satisfaction from playing and spending time with the Grandchildren rather than doing anything else.

Chapter 18:
The Merry Grandchildren

That late night Peter and Mark and Christina stayed up and talked together. They spent precious time together. That night they were happier and exhilarated at being together. They enjoyed their privacy as well as the peace and quiet.

"How is married life? Does it fulfil your expectations?" asked Christina.

"It's great. I love it. I am happily married," replied Peter.

"Isn't it wonderful!" exclaimed Mark.

"Are you going to get married?" asked Peter.

Christina unexplained her intention.

"I don't know. I dream of getting married. I love romance. My parents discourage marriage," answered Christina.

"You will get married. It's inevitable," predicted Peter.

Mark with eager interest did wonder at the Grandchildren.

"How are the Grandchildren? You are spending a lot of time with them," asked Mark.

"These days I have spent time with them. They are great fun. I love them. They are good, sweet and naughty. I love children. I like to be with them. I am a kid at heart. I like to play. I am spending less and less time on my music and more time with the Grandchildren. Due to my commitments and responsibilities, you don't realise what you have got. What you are missing out on."

"I spend my time with my wife. I don't have time for anything else," grinned Peter.

"My wife is in love. I am in love. I hope it reflects in my music," said Mark.

"Why don't you be a nanny? Or do anything with children?" suggested Peter.

"It's a thought. I wouldn't go to that extreme."

"What's that?"

Christina took photographs out of her handbag.

"Before I forget. Let me show you these."

Christina proudly showed photographs of the Grandchildren to Peter and Mark. They both took an interest in looking at it. In one particular photograph both Peter and Mark admired a photograph of a lovely Granddaughter. The Granddaughter was beautifully photogenic dressed up for a night out in London.

Christina showing them was proud of the Grandchildren. From the photographs, the Grandchildren looked ever so merry, exuberant and very happy.

Taking the photographs from each of them. Christina put them back in her handbag. Christina felt tired and sleepy. She got up and came out of the room. Christina retired to bed. She treasured it deeply in her heart!

Chapter 19:

The Band's Discontentment at the Glamour Party

The Band went to a Beverly Hills party. A glamour one. There invited to the party were Artists, Distributors, constellations and galaxies.

The Band relaxed amongst themselves. They sat down together. Everybody mixed around and socialised. The Artists invited had an ego. They were supreme and superior to everybody else. Surpassing everyone else. Others did emulate other Artists.

Everybody at the party drank a glass of Champagne. They talked and socialised. The multimillionaires were conceited, business-like, provocative and snubbers and the glamour Artists extravagant.

Christina envied them. She'd been humiliated, discontented and desirous. Their album sales reached quadruple platinum.

Christina was intent on staying with her group. It deterred anyone from speaking to her. All the best Artists and egotists received all of the limelight and attention.

The glamour host at this party was courtesy of a Record company.

During their short time at the party. The Band talked to a Host rather than anyone else. They eluded them. Preferring to remain together.

Going out in the landscaped garden Christina met an Artist who came up to her. The Male Artist proposed marriage.

"Will you marry me?" Artist asked.

Christina laughed as she found it funny. Christina was overwhelmed at his proposal. His sweet affection. Christina declined his marriage proposal.

"I can't. I am not getting married yet. I wish you well. I will marry you love another time," said Christina nicely.

"I will make sure you keep to your word," muttered Artist.

Christina feeling uneasy walked away. Avoiding everybody else there in the garden. The band full of ego and precaution left the party due to security reasons. Coming outside they got into a luxury limousine parked outside in the drive. The Chauffeur drove them back to their hotel. There Christina relaxed much more in the presence of her own band rather than in a foreign and American location.

Chapter 20:

The Beach House

On the lush island at the beach house, Christina took the time to have a massage. The masseur massaged her body.

She took comfort from her massage. It has a soothing effect.

She self-indulged in erotomania. She took pleasure from her narcissism of eroticism. She felt gratified by her senses. She engaged in narcissistic self-indulgence. Her massage was an over-indulgence. She took pleasure from it.

Christina loved the masseur's gentle touch. Her hands were so soft.

Christina's skin oily. Her body moisturised. The masseur massaging her body. The sporty masseur gave Christina health and beauty tips.

"Do exercise regularly. Do drink fluids. Do eat fresh vegetables and fruit. Do slim. Don't binge. Do moisturise your dry skin with creams."

As soon as the masseur had left, Christina indulged in luxury.

Appreciating deeply the masseur's tips. Christina rested in bed. Her cool room had a ceiling fan. It had exotic plants, bamboo décor and wicker furniture. Outside the surroundings an exotic paradise. The Indian Island a paradisiacal exoticism.

About a few hours later Christina got dressed. She ate succulent fresh fruit and drank exotic fruit juice. She felt an aphrodisiac licking the juice from her lips.

Relaxing alone Christina waited for Peter and Mark to get back. About mid-afternoon Peter and Mark played the guitar and Christina sang beautifully well.

"You will get married," said Peter assuredly.

Mark was convinced without a doubt.

"You will marry."

"I may. I may not. I would like to have a kid," dreamed Christina.

"Oh. You will. There's no stopping you," touched Peter.

"You both have your lives. You have your wives," smiled Christina.

Christina, Peter and Mark came outside to the exotic beach. The white sands and aquamarine sea. They spent time together lounging on the beach. It was a paradisiacal sight of exoticness.

They enjoyed really peaceful times together. It was an exotic, romantic setting or paradise. The scenery was exotic.

"It's a dream!" exclaimed Christina dreamily.

"Aren't we free!" they said joyously.

Christina, Peter and Mark had been beatific, peaceful, carefree and laidback as they took their time to lounge on the beautiful beach.

They idled away their time on the beach every day. They played the guitars and sang, including an acapella.

Chapter 21:

Pep Talk

On Saturday night Peter and Mark came over to see Christina at her house. They all stayed up late and had a heated conversation.

"What are we going to do when our record company drop us," said Christina miserably.

Peter cooled down as he stayed seated.

"I don't know, Christina. Your guess is as good as ours. It's over!" said Peter ashamedly.

"We have failed. It's a flop!" muttered Mark.

"Shall we look for another label?" suggested Peter positively.

"What's the point? We are finished!" said Mark gruffly.

Christina seemed optimistic regardless of failure. "We can still write songs and compose," said Christina optimistically.

"Can we," said Mark sardonically.

Peter hopelessly wondered, "What are we going to do?"

"We have to break up!" replied Christina.

"It's likely we have to," said Mark.

Peter leaned forward. He gestured at Christina.

"What will you do?" asked Peter.

Christina made a witty remark.

"I will elope," joked Christina. "Seriously I will get married. I would like to have a kid. I want to live in a mansion with a nice garden. I would like to travel the world. It's something I have always wanted to do. I will live my life with my Husband. I like to dedicate my life to children. Of course, there will be more to life than just music."

"I will still compose and write songs," said Peter.

"I will quit," said Mark negatively.

This unpleasant conversation made Christina very upset. It felt deeply disappointing and upsetting.

Christina avoided Mark and Peter. She was far too upset to remain in the presence of their company.

She rose and left them both alone in the lounge.

Peter shouted out. He provoked Christina into anger.

"Our company has dropped us. What are we going to do about it?"

Christina felt perturbed in her mind. Going into her bedroom alone. Christina took some time to read her bible. She calmed down. She pacified. Christina still remained disappointed at her Record Company dropping them. The Artists still remained devastated.

Sitting alone together. Peter offered Mark his band member words of encouragement not to give up.

For a few days, Christina went away. She had time to reflect on her disappointment.

Chapter 22:

The Proposition

Peter and Mark came over to Christina's house. They brought their friend a session musician.

Lenny Hubbs strummed his guitar. He played the chords of a new song. Christina sitting opposite Lenny listened to the melody. She took delight in the sweet tune. Lenny played beautifully the guitar.

Christina thought it was too late to use the likes of him. Lenny was apathetic at working on their new material.

Christina admired the guitarist. Peter and Mark approved of the session musician. The professional musician worked on a collaboration.

Mark looked at his wristwatch.

"We must get going," said Mark impatiently.

"You'll be alright," said Peter.

"Yeah man," replied Lenny.

Peter and Mark left Lenny alone with Christina. They had to see their manager.

Lenny practised chords that he composed. Christina admired his professionalism. She clapped her hands.

"I love it. I really love it!" exclaimed Christina

admiringly.

Lenny stopped playing his guitar. He then tuned up his guitar. Paying attention to Christina.

"Will you marry me?" proposed Lenny.

"What!"

"Will you marry me?" repeated Lenny.

"Haven't you asked me this before?"

Lenny made a proposal. "Marry me!"

Christina accepted his proposal. She agreed to marry Lenny.

"Yes. My love. I will marry you."

Lenny and Christina kissed. Their kiss was passionate. It could have been love at first sight!

"When will we set the wedding day?" asked Lenny.

Christina romanticised their wedding.

"Let's not rush. Huh! Let's enjoy it. Shall we?"

Lenny was falling in love. "You'll be my wife. And I'll be your Husband," said Lenny delightedly.

"That's right. We'll be married," smiled Christina.

"Shall we tell them?"

"That can wait. No one needs to know just yet," replied Christina.

"Let's tell."

Christina objected to their proclamation of getting

married.

Within a while, she changed her mind. Then she did phone her best friend to confirm her marriage. Proclaiming she's getting married!

Chapter 23:

The Wedding (Day)

The wedding guests sat down in the church. The three Bridesmaids held the beautiful Bride's wedding dress when going to join the Reverend, Groom and Best Man.

The Reverend took the wedding ceremony. Finally, the Reverend pronounced them both married.

The newlyweds kissed. The newlyweds left the church as the wedding guests standing in the church grounds threw confetti.

The newlyweds hurried to the Chauffeur-driven Rolls Royce which whisked them off.

Later all of the wedding guests attended the reception. The newlyweds sat at the table with their wedding guests. The Husband made a speech.

"Marrying Christina has been the best day of my life. She is my life. My inspiration. I love her so much. Thank you all for making our wedding day a happy one. I and Christina would like to thank everyone involved in our wedding. I can't express how I feel. I am not good at talking. Really I can't. So, I will sing a song."

Lenny picked up his guitar. He played the guitar. Lenny sang a song. Christina sang backing vocals. This love song was appropriate to the occasion. Both Husband and Wife felt so beatific.

Afterwards, all of the wedding guests ate a banquet. The banqueters liked the banquet.

As soon as it was time to depart. The newlyweds went on their honeymoon. The honeymooners honeymooned in the Maldives. The Indian Islands.

The romantic honeymooners had an unforgettable honeymoon. Both Husband and Wife enjoyed their status and their new married life together.

Chapter 24:

The Honeymoon

The Taxi arrived at the hotel. Christina and Lenny went to reception.

The Honeymooners checked in for their reservation. The Receptionist showed them to their hotel room. The porter took their luggage.

Suffering from jet lag Lenny rested in bed while Christina sat down on a chair at the table in the shade. The net curtain was drawn. Christina cooled down in a shady spot. The hotel room cooler in the shade. Christina got up. Christina went out onto the balcony for the first time. There where it was scorching hot. It overlooked the swimming pool. Sunbathers were sunbathing by the poolside and two women were in the swimming pool. Christina was tempted by sensual pleasure. She was gratified by her epicureanism. Christina came back through the patio door. From a Fridge, she took out a bottle of chilled still mineral water. She gulped down some mineral water. Christina felt rather tired, moody and irritable.

She lounged about for hours. She recovered. She felt rather much better from recovering from enervation. She still suffered from jet lag. She desired sexual pleasure tonight.

Later that night Christina dressed up. She applied

make-up. She sprayed perfume on herself. She wore a beautiful black dress. Christina looked ravishingly lovely. Christina was an attractive redhead.

She pleased her Husband who was excited by sexual desire. He desired to make love on their honeymoon tonight.

At a restaurant, the honeymooners dined out. The Diners ate seafood. The epicures indulged. The fresh taste of rich seafood was an aphrodisiac.

"I am in love!" said Wife happily.

"That makes two of us. I am in love too," replied Husband.

"Oh! Good. It's love-making tonight," smiled Wife.

In the candlelight, both honeymooners were deeply romantic and emotional. They both desired love. Desiring passionate love. The ambience was exotic. The exoticism of it a paradisiacal gloriousness. A striking loveliness.

Getting back to their hotel room. They both got undressed. Undressing each other. The Honeymooners made love tonight.

The next day Husband and Wife enjoyed each other's company. They were both madly in love.

They spent time writing lyrics to a song. Lenny played the guitar. Christina sang. Husband and Wife end up singing together. A duet.

They rounded off the day by going to the beach.

They lounged on the sands. Lying down on the sands next to each other.

They heard the sound of the wind blowing. The crushing sound of the sea. Its tide. The atmospheric sensations of it. The waves wash over ashore.

Both Husband and Wife were deeply in love! They enjoyed one another's company. Lenny moved close to his wife. He caressed his wife with loving, passionate touches. They both lay down together alongside each other on the thick white sand. Admiring the exoticness of the beach and the sight of the beautiful sea. It's fine, natural gloriousness. Simultaneously they moved into a supine position. Looking up at the skies. The Honeymooners romanticised.

Getting up from the sand Husband and Wife ran back to their hotel. Going back to their hotel room. They desired to make love. The Honeymooners enjoyed their honeymoon tonight.

In the next few days. Christina and Lenny sang and wrote lyrics together. Lenny was a dedicated musician. His wife Christina was a fine singer. (Nowadays she's disenchanted and demoralised.)

On their honeymoon, they both had a blissful time together.

The Honeymooners had wonderful memories of their Honeymoon. (The married couple recorded a track together when they got back to England, London.)

Chapter 25:

A Christmas Thursday

A parent picked up the Grandchildren and then dropped them off at Christina's house. Christina took pleasure in spending time with the Grandchildren. They enjoyed coming to Christina's house. All of the Grandchildren were excited about Christmas. Christina gave them each assorted chocolates. The Grandchildren loved chocolates. They took delight in their treat.

Christina got great satisfaction in looking after the Grandchildren. Taking care of them remained a responsibility. Nothing else gave her such pleasure, except for her music of course.

Kerry played with her favourite doll and Gerry and Gary played with their soldiers. The Grandchildren loved Christmas. It was seasonal. They became overexcited at Christmastime from either the exciting festivity at their infant or primary school. Today the Grandchildren played indoors rather than outdoors. Today the weather was too cold and chilly. The Grandchildren took enjoyment in playing amongst themselves. They thrilled at the exciting Christmas. None of them really fully understood the true significance of Christmas. The commercialism of Christmas remained worldly materialism.

The children's minds were in a fantasy world of their

own. They possessed their own childish imagination. All they wanted to do was play together.

Lenny spent time with his wife. He did realise how happy his wife had become at being with the Grandchildren. It was another day. It was another Christmas!

Christina admitted. She gained spiritual fulfilment and joy at being with them. She told her Husband how she felt. Her Christmas joy, expectations and fulfilment.

"I do love being with children. Nothing else gives me such joy and pleasure. Of course, the music does. I get such joy at being with the Grandchildren and meeting everyone else's children. This Christmas is truly special. Me spending time with the children is so precious! I am having a wonderful time. The Christmas lives up to my expectations," concluded Christina.

Lenny kissed his wife. Her flushed cheeks reddened from rouge.

"I am glad that you feel that way. It's good to see that you are so happy," said Husband joyously.

Christina experienced a new and different Christmas this year.

"This Christmas is sort of strange and exciting. It is something new."

"Luv, I do hope you have more happy Christmases," wished Husband.

The Grandchildren ended up spending the day at Christina's house. Then they were picked up by their parents and driven home. The Grandchildren thrilled at the excitement of Christmas. This Christmas (glow) was a seasonal enchantment. From the beautiful night, Christmas decorations, Christmas lights and a real Christmas tree.

They took seasonal joy from the wonderful Christmas this year.

The Happy New Year drew closer. They celebrated Christmas and the New Year. A Hogmanay celebration!

Chapter 26:

LA Residence

While Christina's husband spent time playing the guitar with his band, Christina spent time with the glamorous wives. She lounged out in a garden at a Beverly Hills house.

Christina enjoyed the multimillionaire lifestyle. She enjoys her glamorous life. Out in the exotic garden, Christina sunbathed with the wives. She liked her life. Her time of freedom, relaxation and overindulgence.

Her Husband was a jet setter. Christina mixed with the jet set. Christina preferred the American lifestyle to the European way of life. She also did like the other European destinations and locations. (Her Husband was American, so Christina had a preference for America, of course.)

The Californian wives were voluptuaries and materialistic. The worldly-minded wives were epicurean, extravagant and self-indulgent. The rich wives lived a life of overindulgence and self-indulgence. Christina was observant. She had a spiritual insight. Their epicureanism was evident from their habitual tendency for self-indulgence.

Christina was spending time away from England. She enjoyed her time in Beverly Hills. During that week she overindulged in relaxing by the poolside. Her pleasure was an epicureanism. She luxuriated in it, using the amenities provided.

Sunning herself and using luxury beauty products and cosmetics.

Christina used all of the amenities: A sauna, jacuzzi and gymnasium as well as enjoying the available home cinema provided in the mansion. She stayed a few days in LA at one of the wives' houses.

Chapter 27:

Lenny's Breakfast Treat

In the morning Lenny brought his wife breakfast in bed. Christina was delighted with her Husband's treat. Christina appreciated her Husband's thoughtfulness and kindness too.

Christina sat up in bed. She ate a soft-boiled egg and sliced up toast and drank half a cup of tea. She felt refreshed from eating and drinking. Her cheeks glowed.

Lenny standing near a bedpost faced his wife.

"I still don't know what you see in me?"

"You are the love of my life. I love you," said Wife affectionately.

"I love you, babe," said Husband sweetly.

"Will we be together? Or are you going away?"

"Darling. I have to go, I am playing with my band," replied Husband.

"Oh! Do you have to? How about me? Can't you stay with me?"

"Luv! I can't. I have to play with my band. I can't be with you. Peter and Mark send you their best wishes and love."

"I will miss you," munched Wife.

"We will be together," assured Husband.

"Will we. Are you just saying that for the sake of it?"

Christina got out of bed. She hugged and kissed her Husband who stood still. He seemed overwhelmed at his wife's passion. Her passionate kiss. Lenny was already prepared to depart now.

From a bedroom window. Christina stood while watching her Husband leave the house. The Wife had been so upset, tearful and emotional.

Lenny spent a while when waiting outside in the drive. The car arrived on time. Her impatient Husband hurried in a car. He had been whisked away. The band embarked on a Tour.

On Wednesday evening Christina met her ex-band members Peter and Mark at a London Residence. Peter had been kind, polite and accommodating to Christina. Providing her with accommodation. They spent the long night talking together.

"Are you writing any good songs?" asked Peter.

"No. I can't put pen to paper. No words can't express how I feel. Ah! I miss my Husband."

"Lenny is on Tour with the band," said Mark.

"I am sure Lenny misses you. He always does," patted Peter.

Christina felt Peter's gentle pat on her shoulder. Mark touched her hair. She was comforted by his affection. Mark's touching.

"Lenny my love. I love him!" said Christina nicely.

On Christina's birthday, Lenny bought his attractive wife a bouquet of red roses and a diamond ring. Christina expected her Husband's birthday present. It was a nice surprise. Lenny gave his wife a new diamond ring. Christina was overwhelmed with childish delight at his gift. Christina slipped it on her finger. She admired the sparkling diamond ring. The sapphire (ring) was set in a cluster of diamonds.

With joyful appreciation, the wife kissed her Husband. Christina showed him her love.

Lenny celebrated his wife's Birthday with a candlelit dinner at a restaurant. Later Husband and Wife celebrated together with a toast. A Happy Birthday celebration. The merry celebration of his wife's Birthday made up for missed nights.

Later that night Husband and Wife made love!

Chapter 28:
Christina's Values

On that hot day. The blazing sunlight shone through the glass conservatory. The radiance of the sun was dazzling. It was scorching hot.

Together with her Mother in a conservatory. Christina spent time with her Mother. Mother and Daughter perspired in the hot temperature. Christina's Mother fanned herself.

Christina talked about her Husband. Her romantic conversation about her good marriage.

"I do like being married. My marriage to Lenny is great. The only thing I dislike is the fact I just don't see him at times. Other than that, my marriage is wonderful. I do have good sex. He's a good lover. He's such a nice, loving and caring Husband. He's passionate, romantic and generous. I couldn't ask for anything more about him. Me, I am so happy. I am dissatisfied with my music. We could have done much better. When I was much younger, I was single. I had no regrets about being single at the time. As times changed, so did my circumstances change. Marriage was the only option for me. There weren't many prospects or opportunities for me. Getting married to Lenny was the best thing I did. Do I have any regrets? I don't know. I love being married. I loved being a virgin too. Maybe I am nunlike. I do have Irish blood. I am a Catholic. I am a hot-tempered Irish redhead. I am sweet and gentle like a baby."

"I hope your marriage works out," said Mother concernedly.

"I think it will."

"My Daughter is rich," said Mother envyingly.

"I am. We are rich. I have a rich Husband," said Daughter proudly.

"We need your financial help and support," implored Mother.

"Yes. Mom. Don't worry. It will be sorted out," reassured Daughter.

The Mother left her daughter as it was too hot in the conservatory. Her Mother cooled down whilst staying in a cooler room. A cool, shady bedroom.

In the blaze Christina, a dreamer romanticised. She sweltered in the heat. She tanned. Her tanned skin became darker in the scorching heat. The blazing sun became hotter and hotter. She was dehydrated from the rising temperature of the heat.

She marvelled at the gloriously hot weather. She enjoyed it immensely. Naturally, Christina had an obsession with the natural sun as it shone. She was obsessive about tanning herself. A feminine obsessiveness of hers!

She hoped this beautiful, fine weather would last longer. It was another glorious July day!

Chapter 29:

Christina Answers Questions

Christina and her Mother sat in the conservatory. It was full of plants everywhere. It was a natural lovely sight. They both sweltered in the blaze. Cooling down from the light breeze. The cool air was sultry. They were both blinded by the sight of the sun. Sitting at an angle away from the direct natural sunlight. The sunrays scorching. Its resplendence a gloriousness. The glare blinding. Both of them marvelling at the beauty of it. The glorious shining sun. Its radiance.

Slouching on a chair Christina lackadaisical, lethargic and day-dreamy.

"What was the high and low for you?" asked Mother.

"It was when I signed a record contract and got a recording deal. Another great thing about it is the fans. I love my fans. I love it when our fans love us. Meeting all those fans moved me and touching them! I can't explain my emotion. How I feel. The worst thing is writing all those songs and doing all those various demos. What is the point? Leaving my fans and never seeing them again breaks my heart. It breaks all of our hearts," said Daughter honestly.

Christina fidgeted while sitting in her position. She dehydrated, sweated and enervated in the blaze. She felt irritated by her obtrusive Mother making demands. She got irritable with her Mother as she rambled on and from the heat of the sun. At once Christina got up. She left her Mother. Preferring to be all alone.

She went upstairs to her bedroom. She lay down on her bed and rested. She cooled down in the shady coolness of her bedroom.

Resting in bed. Christina thought of her Husband whom she deeply loved!

Chapter 30:

Christina Broods for a Baby

At Christina's house, two children came over to play. (The rich Husband bought his wife the house.)

Lenny desired love from his wife. Christina was too concerned about the children than anything else. The wife loved them and her Husband was fond of them.

"Give me a kiss," demanded Husband with an urge of desire.

The wife kissed her Husband. Her kiss was passionate.

"I love you!" said Wife affectionately.

"I love you. Will we have kids?"

"I am sure we will," replied Wife.

"You love children. You're good with children," said Husband.

"I do love children. Nothing else gives me greater joy," smiled Wife.

"These days you spend a lot of time with these kids. Actually, more time with them than me," said Husband.

"My interest in music has of course diminished. I do have other interests now. I do brood for a baby," said Wife admittedly.

"Why don't we raise a family?"

"Yes. We should. Lenny, you like children. You're a big kid when you play with them."

"Everyone else has kids. Apart from us. Why shouldn't we?" grumbled Husband.

"Do you think you can look after them?"

"Yeah. A proud Father looks after kids."

"You'll make a good Father," remarked Wife.

Going out in the garden. Husband and Wife played with two children playing. They all had a water pistol fight. Both children filled up their water pistols from the filled-up pool.

Everybody got soaked with squirt water. They screamed and shouted. They all had such great fun. Their clothes were wet with squirted water.

Christina got great pleasure and enjoyment at playing with the children. Lenny enjoyed his time playing with them. Christina had a great time looking after the children. Usually, she babysat a Grandchild. Normally she took care of the younger children, especially the Female Teenagers. All of the children adored and loved Christina. They also liked Lenny too.

The children were pampered. A deprived one provided for. They were streetwise and aware of vulnerable and disadvantaged and poor children in a ghetto.

Chapter 31:

Nights and Days

At Christina's house, there were Peter, Mark and their wives present. Christina proclaimed to them. With joyous proclamation.

"I am pregnant! I am an expectant mother."

They all congratulated Christina.

"Congratulations!"

Christina in response acknowledged them politely.

"You're so nice. Thank you!" said Christina politely.

Christina felt unstable as well as unsteady on her feet. She left them together to drink. They had alcoholic drinks from a drinks' cabinet.

Christina joined her caring Husband in the sitting room. Christina lay down on a settee. The Husband sitting by his Wife's small feet. He moved up closer to his wife. He cuddled and caressed his wife.

"If it's a female, I will call her Christine," said Wife passionately.

The Husband acknowledged his wife in response. He was responsive in acknowledgement.

"That's a beautiful name? What if it's a male?"

"I don't know. I haven't thought of a boy's name yet."

Christina felt discomfort and uncomfortable lying on a settee as she's pregnant.

Lenny stayed with his beloved wife. He looked after his wife. He took care of her. He attended to his wife.

The Husband spent nights and days with his wife. Every time in a romantic mood. He loved her. He was concerned for his wife. He worried about her.

Christina felt unwell and anguished. Leaving them together alone.

Peter and Mark and their wives left the house to rejoin their sons and daughters back at their home.

Christina Conceived Her Child

Days and days ago. At the Hospital, Christina gave birth to a healthy, beautiful baby.

Both Mother and baby were well. Christina felt overjoyed at her new born baby. She loved her baby. She admired her baby. A firstborn.

Both Husband and Wife were greatly beatific at their bonny baby.

Christina a Mother called her baby daughter Christine.

The Christening.

At Church on a Sunday morning, there had been a christening. Lenny and Christina's baby, Christine had been christened. The congregation watched the christening.

Chapter 32:

Children's Games

In the bathroom, Christina bathed Christine her daughter in a bath. With a bath towel, the mother dried her daughter. Christina helped her daughter to get dressed.

"Mommy, can I have some sweets?" asked Daughter.

"No. You can't. Too many sweets are bad for you."

"Daddy will give me sweets," tutted Daughter.

"Honey. Stop crying. Or I will send you up to your room," said Mother sternly.

"Mom. I want to play," sulked Daughter.

"Darling. You can play."

Both Mother and Daughter went downstairs. They went out into the garden. There, two children played out in the garden. They were Peter's children. A Son and Daughter. Both children were playful, boisterous, mischievous and extroverted. Christine joined them out in the garden. Christine played with them. The children liked Christine. Christine used to play with them. They were good friends. Mark and Peter's children had a good friendship. They had such good love for one another. They all got on well with everyone.

Looking out of the window Christina observed them.

She watched them play hide and seek out in the big garden.

Christina was a proud Mother. She disliked how her Father went away! Neglecting her Daughter. Christina disapproved of how her Husband neglected Christine.

Watching the children play. Christina was amused at the games they played.

She thought the children's childhood are so precious indeed. She had sweet memories of when she was only a child. Her mind was filled with memories. Christina has good memories.

Going out in the garden. Christina joined them. They all had a water pistol fight. Squirting water from their water pistols at everyone. Christina had such fun. Christine her happy daughter was giggling, playful, childish and amusing. The others that came late there played together for a long time.

During the night Christina conversed with her Mother. At that time Christine her daughter was in bed asleep. Christina talked about her joy of Motherhood. The responsibility of being a responsible parent.

"It's great. I love being a Mother. Having my own Daughter. Nothing else can beat it. Of course, I do love my music. I have always had a passion for music, regardless of anything else. Looking after children. Taking care of them. Christine is my life. My only Daughter. She's everything to me. Nothing else seems to matter."

"It's good you feel that way. You're a parent. You're a good Mother," complimented Mother.

"Gosh! I try. I try to be," sighed Christina.

"Your Husband loves you. Lenny is proud of you," remarked Mother.

"I love my Husband," said Daughter.

"Will your Husband be tempted with having an affair?" said Mother provocatively.

"My Husband is loyal and faithful. He won't do that," said Daughter assuredly.

"I hope not. For your sake!" remonstrated Mother.

Tonight, was an exception. Both Mother and Daughter stayed together for hours. Christina's Mother normally stayed away. Her temperamental and moody Mother envied her Daughter.

Going upstairs to bed late at night, Christina left her Mother downstairs. Going into her Daughter's bedroom. Christina checked on her Daughter sleeping. Her Daughter Christine was sound asleep. The Mother kissed her Daughter on her forehead. Her thick tresses covered her eyes. Her shiny and silky ringlets looked beautiful.

Christina loved her Daughter!

Leaving her Daughter's bedroom. Then Christina went to bed late that night. A midsummer moonlight.

Chapter 33:

Christina Picks up Her Daughter and Her Friend

When it was time Christina drove to College. Reaching the College Christina parked her car in a car park. There she sat waiting for her daughter and her schoolfellow. Then crowds of school children walked by down the path. Christina sitting in the front seat of her car saw two schoolgirls come. The schoolgirls looked lovely in their school uniforms. Christina got out of her car. Christina stood waiting for them to come.

Suddenly Christine ran ahead leaving her friend behind. Christine ran into the outstretched arms of her Mother. The Mother passionately embraced her Daughter. Both Mother and Daughter were passionate and emotional in embracing.

Both schoolgirls got in the car. Christina drove out of a car park and from the grounds of the College. The car reached the end of the road where it gave way to drive down the long road. The car drove past crowds and crowds of school children walking by somewhere down a road. The lolly pop lady accompanied the pedestrians to cross the road.

Reaching home Christine and her friend Rebecca had

tea at Christina's house. Christina treated them. It was a delightful treat. Both Daughter and her friend enjoyed their tea. It was a fine day.

"Christine. How's life in America?" asked Rebecca.

"It's great. My Dad is American. We go to America."

"We have the best of both worlds," added Mother.

"I have never been to America. What is it like? asked Rebecca.

"It's big. The states are rich and poor," answered Christine.

"We love it," said Mother happily.

"We do. I can do country dancing," said Christine impressively.

"Can you really," smiled Rebecca.

"Perhaps I will show you one day."

"Christine loves to dance," said Mother proudly.

"Is it just like the movies?" asked Rebecca.

"Pretty much so," replied Christine.

Rebecca ended up staying an hour at Christine's house. They both relaxed during that time.

Christine's Mother drove Rebecca back home.

At that present time, Christine spent a while looking at herself in the mirror. Standing by a dressing table mirror. Applying make-up on her features.

Christine took narcissism at herself. Christine was a

teenager, a natural beauty! A beautiful schoolgirl growing up!

Chapter 34:
Country Dancing

Christina took an interest in her Daughter as she prepared to practise her country dancing. She practised her dance steps and country dancing. The choreographer did the choreography of a dance scene set to be filmed.

At the country dancing scene, everybody danced beautifully. Christine danced well. The country dancing scene was transcendent and sublime. It was glorious, wonderful, romantic and indeed beautiful the country dancing.

Every dancer was professional. (Christine rehearsed the country dancing scene in a barn.)

The subsequent dance scene earlier was a barn dance which was edited. The filming took place. Everybody who took part in the production was pleased with themselves at how well they danced. This country dancing was taken after a few takes. The cinematographic scenes were truly so beautiful. The cinematography was incredibly wonderful.

The male dancers were American and some females were Latin American. On film, the great country dancing scenes were captured. The midsummer country dancing was shot in a barn.

The filming itself was fabulous. A nostalgia. The country dancing was nostalgic in the way it was filmed. With its cinematography.

Christine kept silent at how she took part in country dancing. Her parents were ever so proud of their Daughter. Both parents were overwhelmed at how well their Daughter danced. Christine's country dancing was brilliant. From all the feedback on their Daughter's rehearsals. A busy schedule.

Chapter 35:

Precious Memories

At home, Lenny arrived with his luggage. He had jet lag from his transatlantic flight.

Lenny burst into the lounge. There he agitated his Daughter.

"Sit down. I want to talk to you," said Father impatiently.

Christina in the kitchen overhead them. Christine obeyed her Father. She sat down in comfort.

"It's over between your Mother and me. I am getting a divorce. I am sorry I have to tell you this. Our marriage is on the rocks," explained Father.

Christine insisted on an explanation.

"Have you found someone? Is that it," scowled Daughter.

"I have found a woman I love! We're having a relationship."

"What about Mom?"

"It's now over between us. I don't love your Mom. I love someone else," said Father emphatically.

"Dad. I am not surprised. I did expect this."

The Father was apologetic towards his Daughter.

"Honey. I am sorry. I really am," said Father apologetically.

Christine could not quite accept her Father's apology.

"Well. It wasn't going to work out."

"You do understand."

"I do, Dad. I do."

"Don't be hard on your Mom."

"Does that mean it's a divorce? Are you separated?"

"We are separated. It's going to be a divorce."

Overhearing the conversation Christina got distraught. With tears in her eyes, Christina ran off. She went upstairs to her double bedroom. She threw herself down on the kingsize bed. Christina began to cry. Christina was deeply unhappy and upset. Her love for her Daughter grew strong. She overcame her disappointment.

Within months Christina dated another man. Christina remarried after years of being divorced. Christina loved her Daughter!

Christine's deep love for Gerry was deeply platonic!

During those short afternoons together, Christine tried to sing as Gerry played the guitar. Kerry possessed a good singing voice. Kerry acquired it from singing practice. Her Mother an experienced singer did the vocal arrangements as well as composing.

On Thanksgiving (Day) Christina, her ex-husband, their Daughter and zealous church members ate a Thanksgiving meal.

They all offered Thanksgiving to God in reverence.

In celebration the Americans celebrated Thanksgiving.

Chapter 36:
Christina's Deep Sentiment

Christina sat out in the shady garden with Kerry, Gerry and Annabel. Christina listened to her Daughter, Christine was a conversationalist and a good listener conversing with Gerry, Kerry and Annabel. Christina was greatly proud of her Virgin Daughter. She loved her Daughter. Christina was wistful and pensive as she engaged in a conversation.

"Is that it! Kerry, you will marry and have kids. The Family tree."

"I will get married," confirmed Kerry. "I will have kids. Then I will be a Mother."

"I am in a steady relationship right now. I am not sure if I am ready for marriage," said Gerry unsurely.

Christine made a childish tut.

"Marriage this! Marriage that! I am a romanticist. I love romance. I have many friends. I am not sure if I want to tie the knot. I love my freedom. I love being a woman. I love female company. I love to sunbathe. I love the continent. I love to travel. I love to dance," expressed Christine.

The Mother had nothing to say but listened to her

Daughter express herself. Christina was too obsessive about her Daughter's Virginity. Her chastity remained intact.

"Christine be good! Do continue with your faith in the Lord. My Dear. You will be blessed. All the blessings of the Lord will come to you," said Mother.

"Yes, Mom. I do share your spiritual principles," acknowledged her Daughter sweetly.

Christina got up from a garden chair. She came indoors. She re-joined Mark who indulged in drinking beer.

"Any regrets?" asked Mark.

"Of course, I have regrets. I have lots of regrets. But what can you do? Anyway, my Daughter means the world to me. I have had a failed marriage. Now I have a good Husband. My Daughter is my life. She means the world to me. I love her so much. Christine is my beautiful Daughter. Lenny used to be my love. My Daughter is my life! She is all that I have left."

Christina expressed her deep sentiment. Christina's sweet affection for her Daughter was touching.

"Christine is your Daughter. You love her so much. She is a blessing. Christine is blessed!" said Mark.

Christina stayed together with Mark today. They both spent precious time together. Their love for each other was strongly platonic, brotherly and sisterly.

Chapter 37:

The Days with Children

Christina allowed her daughter to play with the beach children at her house. These children Christine befriended. Christina got great joy and pleasure at being in the company of children. Nothing else gave her greater joy and pleasure. Except for music. These children playing were playful, good and spiritual. Her Daughter had such fun playing with them out in the garden. Her daughter was a child at heart. Christina entertained the children and got spiritual goodness and wonder at being in the company of children. It was such a great joy. The glory of any good children is the ultimate paradisiacal joy. Christina experienced the beatitude of good, sweet and angelic children. Christina experienced this great feeling since being a Mother to her own Daughter. Christina was attached to the children. She was fond of them. She had a deep love for all of them. Nothing else gave her such joy in her life. Without her Husband, Christina spent days with the beach children. She adored them. Their sweetness, innocence and goodness. These children were adorable and lovable. Christina was overwhelmed at the glorious goodness of the children. They could be good or bad. With her parental love, Christina was motherly. Her Daughter was a typical beach girl. Christina, an experienced Mother took care of the children. She looked after them and disciplined them. One of them was a fan! Another teenager's parents went to Blue Notes. A jazz club. Christina enjoyed their company. Those romantic nights at Blue Notes. Husbands and wives had deep romantic relationships. These romantic married couples were deeply in love. Kissing and holding hands.

Tonight, they had a pleasant night out. They certainly enjoyed the entertainment. It gave them such pleasure and enjoyment. Listening to the brass section of jazz, all of the brass instruments. Listening to all of the brass instruments. Its accompaniment.

Chapter 38:

An Hour At The Beach

At the Balearic Hotel, Christina and her Husband sunbathed together out by the poolside. Their bodies tanned in the heat. Christina enjoyed spending time with her Husband. This may well be the last time with her Husband as he's a jet setter. His peers amongst the jet set. Christina looked at her gold watch. Remembering she was meeting her daughter and the beach children down at the beach. Going to the beach nearby. There she met expectedly her daughter waiting for her at the beach. From there they went down the beach to where the children had built a big, impressive sandcastle. Christina and her Daughter, Christine sunbathed together. Enjoying their leisure. Their time of pleasurable relaxation. The children built a sandcastle. Afterwards, the proud children stood together while admiring the admirable sandcastle. Christine and her mother each took it in turn to take a photograph. They admired the admirable impressive sight of the sandcastle. All the children and Christina and Christine walked home together. The children departed and went home. Mother and Daughter went back to their hotel. They both rounded off the late night by having a Daughter and Mother conversation. They both confided in each other on that Spanish night on the continent. Both Mother and Daughter were beatific while being alone together. Both Mother and Daughter conversed with each other. Their relationship was loving. Mother to Daughter. Their love for each other was a deep love. Both Mother and Daughter conversed out on the dark, shady terrace. Christina and Christine sat facing opposite each other while looking up at the dark sky at night.

NIGHTLIFE

Chapter 1:

Christine's Deep Reflection

Lenny bought his Daughter a lovely house. Out of love the Father treated his Daughter to a big gift.

Years ago, Christine invited Annabel, Gerry and Kerry to her home. They had such a good time together. Christine's mature friends wised up. They were vigilant, spiritual and laid-back. Christine was restful, rejuvenated, regenerated and eagerly desirous.

From the windows, the sun shone with radiance. The heat was sweltering. The light was broad daylight. The room temperature was hot. Cooling down the room an electric fan was left on. The air became cooler from windows left open. The breezy air felt cool.

Christine appeared to be in a happy mood. A jolly, cheerful, good-natured person. Christine and her close friends' voluptuaries, including the beach children who are sybarites were all relaxing together in a restful state. Christine, Annabel, Gerry and Kerry drank a glassful of fresh orange juice. They refreshed from drinking freshly-squeezed orange juice. A few of them munched on cookies.

"What more do you want?" said Gerry unfeelingly.

Christine felt unashamed of being rich. She was used to her Father being amongst the jet set.

"My Father is a musician. He loves me! He cares about me. Why shouldn't he?"

"Your Father has splashed out on you. You do live in a lovely house," said Annabel enviously.

Christine objected to their envy.

"Why shouldn't I live in a nice house, a luxury one?" said Christine unashamedly.

"You're lucky! People can't afford it," said Gerry.

Christine raised an objection, despite their mutual and unspoken agreement.

"I don't give a damn! My Father was once poor. My Father is rich," tutted Christine.

"Don't! There's so much poverty in the world. Isn't there! Millions of poor people. When will it ever end?" said Annabel sympathetically.

With unashamed defiance, Christine spoke out.

"At one time both my parents were poor," said Christine unsympathetically.

"So were ours," they said.

"Aren't rich people poor first before they become rich?" assumed Christine.

"I guess some are," replied Gerry.

"The division. Rich and poor divided," said Christine philosophically.

Annabel responded,

"The poor are in slums, ghettos. Aren't they? The rich burdened with high taxes."

"I am not a sociologist," said Kerry.

"Neither am I," murmured Gerry.

Christine got depressed at this depressing topic.

"Enough of this talk. Let's talk about something else," moaned Christine.

"Hey! Our parents are rich. Shouldn't they enjoy the benefit of it? Their privilege of being rich," said Gerry.

"Quite," uttered Christine.

Annabel, Gerry and Kerry stayed longer together at Christine's luxury house for hours before eventually deciding to leave to go home.

Gerry a driver drove them home. Every passenger. They were lethargic.

At present Christine was alone at home reflecting on her life. Her circumstances. In a calm state when standing by a window, Christine watched a tabby cat roam freely around in the garden. Christine enjoyed the peace. She liked the silence and also her freedom.

Christine in deep reflection contemplated.

"When there's peace and freedom one should make use of it and enjoy it. Don't you think?" thought Christine.

Christine missed her Father. Lenny was divorced and then remarried.

Christine's Mother lived on a Boulevard with her Husband. An American citizen. A Producer.

Did Christine like the American life? She preferred the Spanish lifestyle. Her Mother owned a villa in Mallorca. Christine loved Spain. She loved the Spanish life. The culture, customs, traditions, nightlife, food and drink, music, fashion, Flamenco and beaches.

Christine had a preference for certain beaches. An obsessive love for them. Personally, she had favourite beaches. Christine was obsessed with beautiful beaches. She loved them. Since a girl, she has had a constant obsession with Spanish beaches! She really liked to go to them. It was an obsessional interest of hers. A fascination with her friends. She liked to spend time on a beach. Usually, days there on a beach.

Christine liked to compare her tan with theirs. It was a narcissistic obsession. Her vanity was an obsessiveness! Her tan was a beautiful golden bronze. Their tan was lovely too. Their cheeks glowed. Their complexion of a girlish and woman's beauty. The women's hair was dark, golden, sandy, brown and peroxide red.

Christine stayed out in the garden. She lay down on a hammock. Her body was fully stretched out on it gracefully. She relaxed while lying down. She took comfort as she luxuriated in a position. She felt invigorated by the fresh air. She breathed in the air. Did Christine dream? She didn't dream. She took a nap. The air was cool and breezy. The skies were heavenly. She relaxed in peace. The languor a pleasant niceness. She wished she would never wake up! Her snooze felt ever so beatific and dream-like.

Christine had woken up. Christine began to dance. She danced well. Enjoying her dance. Releasing her inhibitions, she danced. After a short while, she became fatigued. She slouched down on an armchair and rested. She took another nap again. She seemed quite dissatisfied with her dance. Perhaps she would dance better if she was fully recovered from being tired. To regain her fitness.

Christine nodded off for hours. Then when she awoke during that night. Then she went to bed to sleep in comfort, lying down in bed rather than aching in discomfort by remaining sitting on an armchair till early morning.

Chapter 2:
A Toast of the Wedding Anniversary

On a hot summer day, Christine and her friend Annabel swam together in a villa swimming pool.

Christine exhausted from swimming swam to a corner of the swimming pool where she took time to rest. She was out of breath from swimming. Annabel swam past. Showing off her swimming skills. Annabel was lithe, fit and energetic. Annabel swam vigorously.

Christine envied the good swimmer. Annabel swam effortlessly. Annabel did impressive breaststrokes and free strokes in the water. Annabel's tanned body glistened with drops of water. Annabel swam gracefully.

Gerry sat and watched them both swim. He was unenthusiastic about swimming, joining them by the swimming pool.

Staying still in the water. It shimmered in the light. Christine recovered. She regained her breath. She turned and took a look at the virgin swimming. Her impressive strokes in the water. Christine decided to leave them both together. Christine climbed up the steps. Holding onto a rail. Christine came into the villa. She got undressed and showered. She had a lovely hot shower. She took pleasure from her erotomania. She even took narcissism from her eroticism. Her beautiful figure. She turned off the luxury shower. She stepped out of the shower onto a bath mat. Christine reached out for a bath towel on a rail. She dried her body thoroughly. She got dressed. She wore a beautiful black sun dress which left her back exposed. She was beautifully suntanned from sunbathing on the beach day after day.

Christine glanced at her wristwatch. She expected company today. Her Mother, Step Father and Jimmy.

Christine came back out to the poolside. She lay down on a sun lounger. Her body thoroughly dried in the heat. She took the time by waiting for them. Then Christina, her Mother, Step Father, and the producer's son, Jimmy, came as expected to celebrate. They all celebrated together with a glass of Champagne.

Christine celebrated their Wedding Anniversary with a drink. The revellers toasted with a celebration.

"Happy Anniversary!" they celebrated.

Everybody felt moved by the emotional toast. They were standing together toasting in celebration. Drinking each a glassful of Champagne.

After Annabel and Gerry had outstayed their welcome. They all had left the villa. A parent had picked them up and driven them back to the hotel. Christine's Husband drove to a friend's house. His wife was a passenger. (Earlier both Husband and Wife dined at a restaurant.)

Christine sitting in her room reflected on the celebration of her Wedding Anniversary. She appeared to be ambivalent about them celebrating their Wedding Anniversary. Her Father, Lenny, would always be her true Father naturally whatever the case may be.

Christine missed her Father. She became deeply upset thinking of it. She thought her Father had got his own life to live now. Nowadays he was spending fewer and fewer days with his beloved Daughter. Naturally Christine a Mother had custody of her Daughter. (In court it was reported that her Husband was a drunkard!)

Christine was sleeping in bed. She dreamt of her Father. Christine loved her Father. She cried.

The next day Christine showed interest in Jimmy and deep concern for her Father, Lenny. Lying on the sun lounger. She felt discomfort and uncomfortable. She got up. She adjusted the position of the sun lounger. She sat up with her legs stretched out. Christine conversed with her Mother who was lying on a sun lounger next to her. Her Mother flicked through a magazine.

"What's happening with Jimmy and my Father?" asked Daughter.

"Jimmy's Father is a producer. Lenny is believed to be playing the guitar on two tracks. He is the Guitarist," answered Mother.

"Oh! Good! Hey!" exclaimed Daughter beatifically.

Leaving her Mother. She went into the villa. She went to her bedroom. Standing and looking at the dressing table mirror. Christine prepared herself. A vain young woman. Christine changed her girlish hairstyle to a ponytail. It was a plain attractiveness. Also, she applied make-up to her striking features. Since she was a natural stunner with natural skin. She only required a few cosmetics this time.

Later Christine and Annabel went down to the beach together. They enjoyed their time together on the beach. Today this beach was full of holidaymakers. There were sunbathers, families everywhere and little children too playing. With groups of children.

Finding a spot on the beach there Christine and Annabel lounged on the beach for hours. At this present time, they both enjoyed their freedom and pleasure. In mid-afternoon, the glorious sun shone hotter today. They drank fluids, having mouthfuls of still mineral water to quench their thirst. They both took enjoyable pleasure from lying under the parasol together in a sunbathing position. Surrounding them were other sunbathers suntanning themselves.

They took glorious joy at the beauty of the beach. The stunning sea and golden sand.

Going back to the villa. Annabel stayed the night at the villa. Together they both confided in each other. Sitting together that summer night looking at the dark skies tonight.

"It's so peaceful here. It's so beautiful. Where do you get peace like this?" sighed Christine.

"You don't get it anywhere else. Do you. Here is an exception," replied Annabel.

They took delight in the Spanish climate and the too beautiful weather when sitting out on the terrace. They were both dreamy, lethargic and deeply philosophical.

"If it all ends, we've had a wonderful time. Haven't we?" smiled Christine joyously.

"Yes. Indeed. We have. We shall cherish our memories. We shall remember it!" sighed Annabel.

After their philosophical contemplation. They both engaged in a girlie conversation.

"Isn't he handsome!" exclaimed Christine girlishly.

"Yeah. He's dashing."

Christine expressed her irony.

"Oh! We did. Have to miss him. Didn't we!"

"Damn fool!" said Annabel indignantly.

On Thursday morning Christine got quite depressed at thinking of her Father. She did wonder if her Father would come to see her at her Mother's villa. She seemed to think it would be unlikely. She did seem to have wishful thinking!

Christine stayed indoors. She did not go out today. She remained housebound. Christine wanted to be alone. She did not want to see anybody today. She dreadfully missed her Father. When would her Father come to see her?

He made promises to see her which he still did not keep. Christine still loved her Father. She disliked her Step Father. Christine still could not come to terms with how her Mother remarried. Marrying a handsome man who lived in a penthouse. A sound Engineer.

That sultry night Christine could not sleep in bed. She had insomnia. She cried. In bed she was uncovered. In her black lacy nightdress, she sweltered. Her cheeks glowed. The redhead's complexion was ruddy – and peachy.

On Friday afternoon Christine and Annabel went down to the beach again. This time they were unprepared. It was a spur of the moment.

Going down to the lovely beach they had such great fun. They played with the children. They helped the children make a big sandcastle. Each of them used a plastic spade. Christine and Annabel both filled up a bucket with sand. The impatient boys took it. Forcing them to hurry up. The other groups of children built a sandcastle. The sandcastle itself was impressive. The little ones filled a moat with water from the sea.

Christine got such joy, satisfaction and great pleasure at spending time with the excited children. She was fond of every boy and girl. All of the children were excitable about making a sandcastle together. Today was quite a memorable day!

She relived her memory by writing an entry in her personal diary. Sometimes she forgot to make an entry in her diary.

Her friend Annabel liked to read her personal entries in her diary.

Annabel kept a diary herself but made no personal entry in it. Annabel seemed apathetic about it. Annabel was a private person. Furthermore, it was far too personal to keep a diary by making up-to-date entries in it.

Chapter 3:

The Time at an Hour at the Beach

The professional Driver drove the passengers to the beach. Christine's Mother arranged it out of obligation. It was her obligational intention to make arrangements.

Christine and Annabel were excited about being driven to the beach this hot afternoon. They both wore sundresses which were slinky and sheer.

Reaching near the beach the attractive women got out of the car. They closed the car door and both waved at the Driver in appreciative acknowledgement. Both young women agreed to meet the Driver at the same place near the grounds of the beach. Both women had virginal beauty. The ostentatious and flamboyant virgins paraded. They walked within reach of the beach. There were families, children and sunbathers on the golden beach. They both attracted attention. They did enjoy the attention they both received. Both virgins were puritanical and pious. They both looked down on the prurient sunbathers.

Walking down along the beach. They were admired, adored and revered by mostly everybody.

The oglers admired them.

Adoring the virgins who were sanguine and sanctimonious. Their nature was a virtue!

There the children playing on the beach did not pay attention to them or anybody else at all at that time.

Going somewhere down the long beach they were both overwhelmed with joy by attracting attention. The oglers admired them and lechers adored them.

Reaching farther up the beach they both came across señoritas. One of them wore a beautiful Spanish red dress and another one a friend of hers a black dress.

Both women smiled while walking past the sleek and chic señoritas. Their shiny, long hair looked so beautiful! They both admired them with the deepest respect. Having deep love and regard for the Spaniards.

Christine and Annabel turned back and walked back to the grounds of the beach. There where they both waited for the Driver to pick them up. They both had a wonderful day!

That summer was unforgettable!

Chapter 4:

Religious Beliefs

Christine, Annabel and Gerry stayed in a villa while Christina and her Husband embarked on a Day Trip today.

They stayed together in a villa. Enjoying each other's company. They all had a good friendship. Together they had a pleasant time.

Christine sat down with Annabel and Gerry. She conversed with them. She reflected on her glamour days.

"My life has changed. It's no longer glamorous. It's less and less glamour," frowned Christine.

"Your parents are remarried. Isn't that so?" stated Gerry.

Christine objected to her parents getting remarried. She disapproved of it.

"In my crazy state. I don't know if I have gotten over it. There have been changes to my life. My parents discourage me from having parties. My Father has his wild parties."

"Life just isn't the same anymore. It has changed," groaned Annabel.

Gerry has regenerative ideals.

"Aren't we spiritual in our outlook?" said Gerry regeneratively.

"We are spiritual," said Christine surely.

"Call us sensible. That's what," said Annabel loudly.

Gerry clenched his fist.

"We are spiritual. We are Believers," said Gerry joyously.

Christine engaged in deep regeneration.

"My Mother is a Catholic. I suppose she is," said Christine proudly.

They had illumination and enlightenment of their deep spirituality.

"We live good lives. We are not bad. Are we?" pointed out Gerry.

"It's a good thing. We are spiritual. For our sakes," reassured Christine.

"Hey! Temptation!" retorted Annabel.

With reassurance Christine restored faith.

"That won't affect me, us if we are believers. Will it?" said Christine assuredly.

"Our parents insist on us living good lives," said Annabel.

"Yes. They do," murmured Gerry.

"Our lives depend on it!" said Christine spiritually.

They engaged in a deep spiritual conversation.

"We must live good lives. We must be prayerful. We must keep away from worldly things. But be spiritual," insisted Christine.

"I quite agree. Our love for the Lord. Is the way forward. Isn't it!"

"It is the ultimate," proclaimed Annabel.

"The older we become the more faith we have, don't we? We do have a spiritual outlook in our lives," said Christine positively.

As a result, certain individuals disapproved of them. They rejected people, non-believers. The Damned! As they seemed to think of them as being just religious. With good faith, they all had deep spiritual conversations. They shared and exchanged their religious beliefs and faith.

"The condemned will be damned. That's it! That's how it will be," concluded Christine affirmatively.

"Yeah. Strong stuff," slurred Annabel.

"Without doubt. You're right," agreed Gerry.

"Exactly!" they said.

Regarding everybody else, they all kept quiet about their faith to avoid persecution and apologetics as well as being apolitical. The others certainly may have been indifferent to their faith.

Chapter 5:
Nightlife

On the following nights Christine, Annabel and Gerry went to a nightclub, wine bar, art gallery and restaurant.

They enjoyed the Spanish nightlife, as well as the touristy hotspots. (This time last year they went to scenic Ibiza. There they marvelled at the beautiful Islands including the Balearics.)

In a strange way, Christine remained camera shy. No photographs of her had been taken anywhere, especially in Ibiza because of Christine's superstition, her superstitious ways. There she dreamt of the Spanish Island. She had wonderful dreams!

Chapter 6:

A Private Location

On the Island, Christine and Annabel stayed at a luxury hotel. Both voluptuaries spent time together in a luxury pool. The walls were made of thick stone. Thereabouts the surroundings were private. It faced the Mediterranean Sea.

Both women indulged in a glassful of fruity Champagne. They ate pieces of fresh fruit. The Epicures indulged. They indulged in epicurism and epicureanism. The Epicureans' aphrodisiac.

After the sybarites had such fun. They engaged in sensual pleasure. They had such a peaceful time together. Both women took pleasure in their eroticism and erotomania. They had great excitement and pleasure. Christine and Annabel enjoyed their time together. The virgins were overwhelmed with joy. Splashing in the water. Spending time with the one which they deeply loved.

The paradisiacal location was so stunningly beautiful! It was a dream paradise.

Chapter 7:

The Reconciliation

One day at the villa, Lenny came to see his beloved Daughter. As soon as Christine saw her Father, she jumped up in joy. She exclaimed in surprise, "Father!"

Christine expected her Father. She anticipated the emotional reconciliation between them.

Christine ran and threw her outstretched arms around her Father. Both Father and Daughter were deeply passionate and emotional. Their reconciliation was so passionate. Both reconcilers embraced tenderly. Christine cries in the arms of her passionate Father.

———————

*Available worldwide from
Amazon and all good bookstores*

www.mtp.agency

www.facebook.com/mtp.agency

@mtp_agency

www.ingramcontent.com/pod-product-compliance
Lightning Source LLC
LaVergne TN
LVHW011719060526
838200LV00051B/2951